Ash and Eddy took 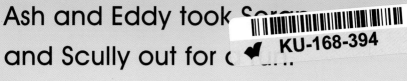 Scully out for a...

"Take them off the lead,"
said Ash.

4

He threw a
stick for them.
It was a good
game.

"Here Scully!" shouted Ash.
"Leave it now, Scrap!"
called Eddy.

6

But the dogs did not
even look back.

Scully saw a ball. "Don't chew the ball!" shouted Ash.

Oh dear!

Scully ran on.

Scrap saw a duck.
"Don't chase the duck!"
called Eddy.

Oh dear!

The duck flew away
but Scrap ran on.

The dogs saw some thick
sticky mud.
"Please stay out of the mud.
Keep clean!" shouted Ash.

Scrap and Scully ran on.
They went over a gate

and came to a stream.

Scrap went splash!

Scully went splash!

The boys got to the stream.
"I can leap over it!" said Ash.

Ash flew along but...

Splash!

Scrap and Scully came back.
Eddy got them on the lead.
"No more 'run-away game'
for you!" he said.

Oh dear!

Puzzle Time

Find the six sound pairs!

One has been done for you.

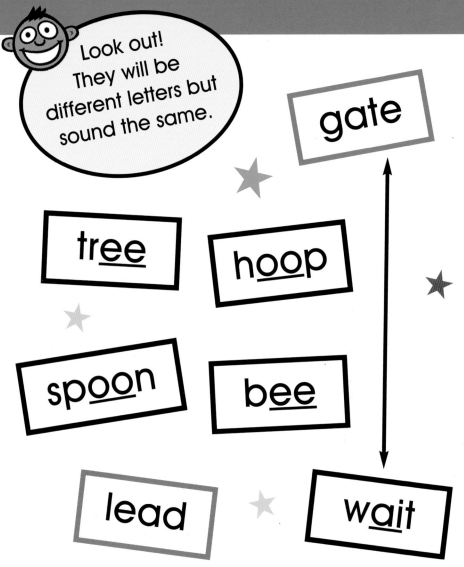

Look out! They will be different letters but sound the same.

gate

tree

hoop

spoon

bee

lead

wait

screw

even

m<u>ai</u>l

flew

chase

Answers

wait – gate is already completed to show the first pair.

chase and **mail** are also both **/ai/**
bee, tree, even, lead are all **/ee/**
hoop, flew, screw, spoon are all long **/oo/**

A note about the phonics in this book

Concentrating on new phonemes
In this book children practise reading new graphemes (letters) for some phonemes (sounds) that they already know. For example, they already know that the letters ee make the /ee/ sound but now they are practising that ea and e-e can also make the /ee/ sound.

Known phoneme	New graphemes	Words in the story
/ai/	a-e	came, chase, late, gate, take
/ee/	ea	stream, please, lead, leave, leap, clean
/ee/	e-e	these, even
/oo/	ew	threw, chew, flew
common words	here, came, don't	
tricky common words	called	

Remind children about the letters they already know for these phonemes.

In the puzzle they are challenged to match the words that have the same sound in them; the same sound but different letters.

Top tip: if a child gets stuck on a word then ask them to try and sound it out and then blend it together again or show them how to do this. For example, stream, s-t-r-ea-m, stream.